DATE DUE

SEP 2 3 2013			

Writing Builders

Leah and LeShawn Build a
LETTER

by Rachel Lynette
illustrated by Steve Cox

Content Consultant
Jan Lacina, Ph.D.
College of Education
Texas Christian University

NORWOOD HOUSE PRESS
CHICAGO, ILLINOIS

Norwood House Press
P.O. Box 316598
Chicago, Illinois 60631
For information regarding Norwood House Press, please visit
our website at:
www.norwoodhousepress.com or call 866-565-2900

Editor: Melissa York
Designer: Christa Schneider
Project Management: Red Line Editorial

Library of Congress Cataloging-in-Publication Data
Lynette, Rachel.
 Leah and Leshawn build a letter / by Rachel Lynette ; illustrated
by Steve Cox.
    p. cm. -- (Writing builders)
Includes bibliographical references.
 Summary: "Two friends learn to write letters to a classmate
who has moved away"--Provided by publisher.
 ISBN-13: 978-1-59953-510-4 (library ed. : alk. paper)
 ISBN-10: 1-59953-510-6 (library ed. : alk. paper)
 ISBN-13: 978-1-60357-390-0 (e-book)
 ISBN-10: 1-60357-390-9 (e-book)
 1. Letter writing--Juvenile literature. 2. English language--
Composition and exercises--Juvenile literature. I. Cox, Steve,
1961-, ill. II. Title.
 PE1483.L96 2012
 808.6--dc23
                          2011038970

Manufactured in the United States of America in North
Mankato, Minnesota.
195N—012012

Words in **black bold** are defined in the glossary.

Writing Letters Is Fun!

I really miss Tyler, my best friend. Tyler used to live on our street, but he moved away a few months ago. We have known each other since kindergarten. We used to do everything together.

Then last week, my friend Leah had a great idea. She said we should write a letter to Tyler. I had never written a letter before, but Leah showed me how. It's easy and fun! Writing a letter is different than talking on the phone because you can think about exactly what you want to say.

Here's the best part: Today I got a letter from Tyler! It is really fun to get a letter in the mail!

LeShawn, age 8

Leah climbed into the car. "What a close game!" she exclaimed.

"Sure was. I bet we would have won if Tyler had been here," replied LeShawn as he rolled down his window. "He hit four home runs last season."

"He's a good pitcher, too," said Leah. As the car started to move, Leah looked out the window thoughtfully. "I wonder if he plays on a baseball team in his new town."

"Hey, I have an idea! Why don't we write him a letter? Maybe he will write back and tell us about his life in Oregon," said Leah excitedly.

"Do you have his address?" asked LeShawn.

"I have it," Leah's mom, Mrs. Dunway, chimed in from the front of the car. "I have some **stationery** you can use, too."

"Stationery? What's that?" asked LeShawn.

"Stationery is paper that people use to write letters," replied Leah.

"Can't we just use notebook paper?" asked LeShawn.

"You can, but stationery makes the letter more special."

When Leah and LeShawn got back to Leah's house, they sat down at the dining room table. Mrs. Dunway gave them light yellow stationery with smiley faces in the corners. There were matching envelopes, too.

"I see what you mean about how stationery makes the letter more special," said LeShawn. "So what do we do first?"

"Here's a notebook," said Mrs. Dunway. "Why don't you start by thinking about what you want to say in your letter. Then you can write it down. It will help you organize your thoughts before you use the stationery."

"I want to tell him all kinds of things," said LeShawn excitedly. "A lot has happened since he moved! There was the science fair, playing baseball, the field trip to the zoo . . . oh, and Andrew broke his leg and . . ."

"That's a lot for one letter!" exclaimed Leah. "Let's write everything down and then decide what the most important things are."

science fair
baseball game
new kid in our class
field trip to the zoo
Andrew broke his leg
went to the movies
LeShawn's new puppy

Leah's birthday party
school play
Valentine's Day party
got a new video game

"Okay, now we have a pretty good list," said Leah. "Letters can be as long or short as you want. Since you're new to letter writing, let's pick three important things to write about."

"Well, some of this happened a long time ago, like the Valentine's Day party and the school play," said LeShawn. Leah crossed those ideas off the list.

"And Tyler might not be that interested in some of these things," added Leah. "We could cross off the movies, the video game, and the new kid in class."

"I don't want to write about the baseball game because we lost! Let's write about the zoo, your birthday party, and my new puppy," decided LeShawn.

"So now I know what I want to write about," said LeShawn. "What do we do next?"

"Here, look at this letter I wrote to my grandma. I was going to mail it later." Leah pulled an envelope out of her pocket, took out a letter, and unfolded it carefully.

"My mom helped me write it," Leah continued. "She showed me how a letter has five parts. There is the **heading** at the top of the letter, the **greeting**, the **body** of the letter, the **closing**, and the **signature**."

52476 Elm Street
Park Ridge, IL 60068
May 16, 2012

Dear Grandma,
　　Thanks for your last letter! I was glad to hear that you and Grandpa planted flowers in the front yard. It will be fun to see them when we come to visit in July.
　　My project won second place at our school science fair! Dad helped me to make a circuit with batteries and bulbs. I explained all about how electricity works.
　　Please give Grandpa a hug for me and write back soon.

Love,
Leah

Dear Tyler

52522 Elm Street
Park Ridge, IL 60068
May 18, 2012

"So, we start with the heading at the top and on the right side of the page?" asked LeShawn.

"Yes. The heading includes your address and the date," answered Leah.

LeShawn wrote:

52522 Elm Street
Park Ridge, IL 60068
May 18, 2012

"Oh, now I see why the heading is important. It lets Tyler know our address so he can write us back," said LeShawn. "It looks like the greeting is next." LeShawn started a new line and wrote:

Dear Tyler,

"Don't forget the comma," said Leah. "The greeting always ends with a comma."

LeShawn added the comma. "Now what?"

"Now we write the body of the letter. The body is everything you want to say to Tyler."

Mrs. Dunway walked into the dining room with a tray of carrot sticks with vegetable dip and two glasses of milk. "You could try an introduction," she added. "That's where you tell the other person why you're writing the letter."

"That makes sense," said LeShawn, starting to write. "How about this?" LeShawn showed Leah and Mrs. Dunway the letter.

52522 Elm Street
Park Ridge, IL 60068
May 18, 2012

Dear Tyler,
    Today Leah and I were remembering how much fun we had last year when we were all on the same baseball team. We decided to write you a letter to tell you what has been happening since you moved.

"You two reminded me that there are some letters that I need to write, too," said Mrs. Dunway.

"Really?" asked LeShawn. "Do you have a friend who moved away?"

"Not exactly," said Mrs. Dunway. "Letters are helpful for many reasons. I need to write a thank-you letter to my aunt for a gift that she sent me. I'd also like to write the mayor a letter asking the city to put a stop sign on the corner at the end of our block."

"You can write a letter to the mayor? Wow!" said LeShawn.

"Sure, you can write a letter to just about anyone if you have their address—an author, an athlete, even the president! I like writing to authors because they almost always write back," said Leah. "But we need to finish our letter to Tyler first."

Leah and LeShawn worked together to write about their class field trip to the zoo. They started writing about Leah's birthday next.

Leah picked up the page and read what they had written. "I think we need to fix something. We talked about the field trip to the zoo, and then we started talking about

my birthday party. Since my birthday is a new subject, we need a new paragraph."

LeShawn erased the last sentence he had written and rewrote it in a new paragraph. By the time they had written about Leah's birthday party and LeShawn's new puppy, the carrot sticks were gone.

23

"We're almost done now, right?" said LeShawn as he put the period after the last sentence.

"Almost," replied Leah, "but we still need a conclusion. That way it doesn't end suddenly. How about: We really miss you. Please write back soon and tell us all about your life in Oregon."

"Perfect," said LeShawn. "Now we need the closing and the signature, right?"

"Right!"

"Okay, but I don't want to sign it 'Love' like you did with your grandma. Can we write 'From' instead?"

"We could," said Leah, "but another closing might sound better. I use 'Sincerely' when I write to an author, but that doesn't sound quite right."

"What about 'Your friends,'" suggested LeShawn.

"Good idea!" said Leah. "Remember that the closing and the signature go on the right side of the paper like the heading."

LeShawn wrote the closing. This time he remembered the comma at the end. They both signed the letter. "That was fun," said LeShawn as he read over the letter.

52522 Elm Street
Park Ridge, IL 60068
May 18, 2012

Dear Tyler,

Today Leah and I were remembering how much fun we had last year when we were all on the same baseball team. We decided to write you a letter to tell you what has been happening since you moved.

Last week our class took a field trip to the zoo! I liked the monkeys the best. Leah liked the giraffes. Have you gone on any field trips with your new class?

Leah's birthday party was really fun too! She had a bowling party. I got two strikes! The cake was in the shape of a bowling pin and it was chocolate, yum!

I finally got a puppy! We named him Cody. How does Daisy like your new neighborhood? I bet if you still lived here, Cody and Daisy would be good friends.

We really miss you. Please write back soon and tell us all about your life in Oregon.

Your friends,
LeShawn and Leah

Mrs. Dunway gave them a stamp for the envelope. Leah carefully wrote Tyler's name and address on the front of the envelope. Then she wrote LeShawn's address on the upper left-hand corner of the envelope. "This is called the return address, " she told LeShawn. "That way, if your letter doesn't get to where it is supposed to go, the post office can send it back to you."

He put the stamp in the upper right hand corner. "Let's mail it right now!"

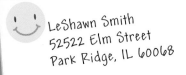

LeShawn Smith
52522 Elm Street
Park Ridge, IL 60068

Tyler Jones
2555 Park View Street
Portland, OR 97225

You can write a letter, too!

Who do you want to write your letter to? You can write to someone you know, like a friend or a relative, or you can write to someone you have never met, like an author, a movie star, or an athlete.

A letter has five parts: the heading, the greeting, the body, the closing, and the signature. It is a good idea to write down some ideas about what you want to say before you write the body of your letter. Then pick a few favorites to write about. If you are writing to a friend or a relative, you might want to write about what is going on in your life. If you are writing to someone you do not know, you will want to start your letter by telling that person why you are writing. You may also want to ask the person some questions.

Try writing a letter to someone famous. What do you want to tell that person? What do you want to ask? Remember to use a new paragraph when you change subjects. Here is a letter that Leah wrote to one of her favorite authors. Read her letter, and then write a letter to someone that you admire.

52476 Elm Street
Park Ridge, IL 60068
April 14, 2012

Dear Ms. Robbins,

I am writing to tell you how much I enjoyed reading *Lemonade Summer*. It is one of my favorite books and I have told all of my friends to read it.

My favorite part of *Lemonade Summer* was when Lizzy woke up on the second morning to find that there were already hundreds of people in line at her lemonade stand. I thought it was really funny when she ran outside while she was still in her pajamas!

I would like to be an author too when I grow up, but sometimes I have trouble thinking of good ideas for a story. How do you get the ideas for your books? How did you get the idea for *Lemonade Summer*?

Thank you for reading my letter and for writing such wonderful books!

Sincerely,
Leah Dunway

Glossary

body: the message of the letter.

closing: a word or phrase, followed by a comma, to end the letter.

greeting: the opening, followed by a comma.

heading: your address and the date at the top of the letter.

signature: your name signed under the closing.

stationery: special paper used for writing letters.

For More Information

Books

Jarnow, Jill. *Writing to Correspond*. New York: PowerKids Press, 2006.

Teague, Mark. *Dear Mrs. La Rue: Letters from Obedience School*. New York: Scholastic, 2002.

Tellegen, Toon. *Letters to Anyone and Everyone*. London: Boxer Books, 2009.

Websites

Letter Generator
http://www.readwritethink.org/files/resources/interactives/letter_generator/

Fill in the blanks to create all five parts of a letter that you can print.

Letters To . . .
http://pbskids.org/arthur/games/lettersto/

Select phrases to create a fun letter to one of the characters from the PBS show *Arthur*.

About the Author

Rachel Lynette has written more than 100 books for children of all ages as well as resource materials for teachers. When she isn't writing she enjoys spending time with her family and friends, traveling, reading, and drawing.